c.1

398
BRE

Brenner, Barbara

Little One Inch

DATE			
T-104			
JAN 1 1 '90	104		
MAR 1 4 '91	101		
APR 1 7 '91	206		
FEB 1 2 '92	105		

© THE BAKER & TAYLOR CO.

LITTLE ONE INCH

by Barbara Brenner

illustrated by Fred Brenner

Coward, McCann & Geoghegan, Inc. / New York

To my dad

Library of Congress Cataloging in Publication Data/Brenner, Barbara. Little One Inch. A new version of the Japanese fairy tale Issunbōshi. Summary: Although he is only an inch tall, Issun Boshi cleverly defeats several demons. [1. Fairy tales. 2. Folklore—Japan] I. Brenner, Fred. II. Issunbōshi. III. Title. PZ8.B6738Li [398.2] [E] 76-45434 Printed in the United States of America

About this story

Readers who know this ancient folk tale may notice the addition of two characters to the story—the *Tengu* and the *Kappa*. These are both demon figures which come directly out of Japanese mythology, where they have occupied an honored place for centuries. However, in researching this book, we discovered that demons change both their form and their personalities as they move through history. Storytellers and artists add their own personal vision of the *Oni,* nobleman, and Issun Boshi. Demons are sometimes wicked, sometimes merely mischievous. A *Kappa* may in one century be a creature with a tortoise body and a child's head, while in another it is a monkey with the scales of a fish. A *Tengu* is a mischievous birdman at times. In other stories it is an evil feathered devil with a long nose.

So, we have had to make choices. And this new version of *Little One Inch,* while it is based on authentic source material, is also the personal voice of the writer and the artist, taking from the past and shaping the old legend in a new way.

*I*n Japan a fairy tale often starts with the words Mukashi mukashi, which means "Long, long ago." Since this story was suggested by Japanese folk tales and legends, it begins in the Japanese way...

Mukashi mukashi there lived a farmer and his wife. They had no children and they wanted a child very badly. One day the woman went to the local shrine and prayed to the gods for help.

"Give us a child," she pleaded. "Just one small child to love and cherish. I would not care even if it were no bigger than a finger on my hand."

The gods smiled. Soon the woman found that she was to have a child.

When the baby was born, he was perfectly formed in every way, except that he was exceedingly small. He was, in fact, no bigger than a finger. Nevertheless, his parents were delighted. They named him *Issun Boshi,* which means "Little One Inch."

The years passed. Issun Boshi grew older, although he never grew much bigger. The time came when he was a young man, old enough to leave home and travel down the river to seek his fortune in the big city of Kyoto.

His parents helped him to get ready.

His mother made him a fine little suit from a silk handkerchief.

His father made him a sword from a sewing needle and a sword case from a hollow straw.

They gave him a rice bowl for a boat and a pair of chopsticks for oars.

Now Issun Boshi was ready to journey to Kyoto. But before he left, his mother and father warned him of the dangers he faced out in the world beyond the farm.

"You are small," they said, "so you must be clever. Watch out for strangers with heavy boots. Watch out for wagon wheels and animals with sharp teeth. Above all, beware of demons. They are everywhere in the great outside world."

"What are demons and how will I know them?" Issun Boshi asked his parents.

"The *Kappa* is a river demon," they told him. "It lives under the water and does not see very well. It has the face of a monkey and the feet of a frog. The Kappa will try to pull you into the water, where it will eat you up."

"The *Tengu* is another demon. It has the body of a man and the head of a bird. Tengu will play tricks on you, steal from you, and harass your journey. They are also very curious."

"But the fiercest demons of all are the Oni. Oni are giants whom you will know by their horns and their magic hammers. Oni never cry real tears, so they can never feel pity."

Issun Boshi promised he would remember the words of his parents. He climbed into his rice-bowl boat and pushed off from shore. Soon his mother and father and the farm were out of sight.

The little boat and its tiny passenger floated down the river. From time to time Issun Boshi took a stroke with the oars to steer. When the sun was high, he stopped among some water lily pads to eat his lunch. He had swallowed a bit of fish and a few grains of rice and was just about to take a bite of cucumber when a voice said,

"Ho there! Who wants to play pull-finger with me?"

Issun Boshi looked over the side of the boat. There in the water was a creature with the face of a monkey and the feet of a frog. A Kappa!

"Play pull-finger with me!" the Kappa whined. "I will try to pull you in and you try to pull me out!"

Remembering his parents' words, Issun Boshi held the cucumber over the side of the boat. The Kappa pulled on it, thinking that it was a finger. All of a sudden, Issun Boshi let go. The Kappa grabbed the cucumber and disappeared under the water, where he gobbled it up.

While the Kappa was eating, Issun Boshi rowed quietly away.

He drifted downstream toward Kyoto. When night came, he pulled into shore and lay down in the boat to sleep. He had just closed his eyes when he heard a rustling in the pine trees. He looked up and saw a flock of birds. Birds with the bodies of men!

"Tengu!" whispered Issun Boshi.

He could hear them talking.

"Let us trick this tiny young man," one said.

"We'll pick him up and splash him in the river!"

"Steal his oars so he cannot steer his boat!"

Issun Boshi pretended not to hear them. Remembering his parents' words, he drew his sword and cut a piece of bamboo from the water's edge. The Tengu watched, curious, as he knew they would be. Putting the hollow stem to his eye, he gazed up at the sky. Soon a Tengu called,

"What are you doing down there?"

"I'm looking through my magic reed," Issun Boshi answered. "With it I can see all the wonders of the heavens."

"Wonders of the heavens? We should like to see that," said another Tengu. "Give it to us this minute!"

"Very well," said Issun Boshi. "I will throw it up to you."

He threw the piece of bamboo far into the woods. All the Tengu flew off, shrieking, to find the "magic" reed. By the time they discovered Issun Boshi's trick, the tiny young man was far away.

The next day Issun Boshi arrived in Kyoto. He walked about all day in the bustling city. Several times he was in danger from wagon wheels and strangers' boots and once from an

animal with sharp teeth. But he remembered his parents'
words and got through the day safely.

At nightfall he came to a large and beautiful house at the
edge of the city. Issun Boshi walked through the gates and
knocked at the door. When it opened he called, "Here I am!"
as loudly as he could. He found himself looking up into the
kind face of an elderly merchant.

The merchant scooped him up on his fan and said with a smile,

"Well! What have we here?"

"I am Issun Boshi," said the tiny young man. "Although I am small, I am brave and clever. I have already outwitted two demons." He told the man the story of his journey and asked for work.

The merchant was pleased to meet such a clever young fellow. He told Issun Boshi he could stay in his house and act as bodyguard for his beautiful daughter, Michiko.

So Issun Boshi came to stay with the merchant and he soon became a favorite with everyone. He and Michiko were never happier than when they were in each other's company.

Several months went by. Issun Boshi had almost forgotten about demons. One day he and the merchant's daughter were on their way to market when two giants with horns and hammers appeared out of nowhere.

Instantly Issun Boshi remembered the warning of his parents.

"Oni!" he cried. He drew his tiny sword, prepared to defend the girl. But before he could strike a blow, one of the Oni snatched him up and swallowed him.

It was dark in the Oni's belly. At first Issun Boshi could not see. As soon as his eyes were used to the darkness, he began to slash about with his sword. Slipping and sliding, he worked his way up the Oni's gullet.

Meanwhile, both giants had seized Michiko and were about to carry her off when one of the Oni suddenly clutched his chest. The little needle sword had found its mark.

The Oni gave a tremendous groan and spit out Issun Boshi. He immediately sprang into the eye of the second Oni. Suddenly the Oni's eye began to tear. And the moment that he cried real tears, the Oni felt pity for the merchant's daughter and released her.

The two Oni ran away. But in their haste they dropped their magic hammers.

"Look there!" cried Michiko. "The Oni have left their magic hammers. If we strike the hammers on the ground and make a wish it will come true."

"Let us each make a wish then," said Issun Boshi.

"What will you wish?" the young woman asked him softly.

"I shall wish for us to be the same size, so that we may marry. For I love you and want you to be my wife."

"That is my wish, too," said Michiko. "I love you and I want to be with you always."

The sound of hammers striking rang out on the morning air.

Once again the gods smiled. The merchant's daughter and the tiny young man became the same size!

So they were married. And they lived happily to a ripe old age in a tiny house just right for two people no bigger than fingers on a hand.